To Katy Mackall, April Coffman,
Melissa and Michelle Kinney,
who love those cookies!

—DDM

To Rebekah Marie.......welcome!

—RC

ZONDERKIDZ

*The Legend of the Christmas Cookie*
Copyright © 2008 by Dandi Daley Mackall
Illustrations © 2015 by Richard Cowdrey

Requests for information should be addressed to:
Zonderkidz, 3900 Sparks Drive SE, Grand Rapids, Michigan 49546

This edition: ISBN-13: 978-0-310-74767-3

Library of Congress Cataloging-in-Publication Data

Mackall, Dandi Daley.

     The gift of the Christmas cookie : sharing the true meaning of Christmas
/ by Dandi Daley Mackall ; illustrated by Richard Cowdrey.
     p. cm. --
Summary: During the Great Depression, Jack helps his mother make cookies for the needy at their church, learns the story
of how the first Christmas cookies were used to spread the gospel to people who could not read, then finds a way to bring
that story to life.
     ISBN-13: 978-0-310-71328-9 (jacketed hardcover)
     ISBN-10: 0-310-71328-5 (jacketed hardcover)
     1. Cookies-Fiction. 2. Christmas-Fiction. 3. Generosity-Fiction.
4. Depressions-1929-Fiction.]   I. Chabrian, Deborah L., ill.  II. Title.
PZ7.M1905Gif 2008
[E]--dc22                                                    2006027611

*Editor: Barbara Herndon*
*Art direction and design: Kris Nelson*

*Printed in China*

15 16 17 18 19 / LPC / 21 20 19 18 17 16 15 14 13 12 11 10 9 8 7 6 5 4 3 2 1

# The Legend of the Christmas Cookie

## Sharing the True Meaning of Christmas

WRITTEN BY Dandi Daley Mackall     ILLUSTRATED BY Richard Cowdrey

ZONDERkidz

**I**n the distance Jack heard the lonely cry of a train whistle. He leaned into the icy wind and crossed the railroad tracks toward home.

*Home.* Their house hadn't felt like a home since Jack's dad had hopped a freight train West to find work. Now, on Christmas Eve, word came that Dad couldn't make it home for Christmas.

As Jack stepped inside, the heavenly scent of sweet bread and licorice wafted from the kitchen. *Cookies!*

But it couldn't be. Mom put every penny Dad sent home straight into the cookie jar. There hadn't been a single cookie in that jar for over a year.

"Jack?" Mom called. She was in the kitchen, stirring something in a giant bowl.

"You're really making cookies?" Jack still couldn't believe it.

His mother smiled weakly. "They're for the needy at church."

Jack tried to hide his disappointment. He'd been feeling pretty needy himself lately.

"Unpack the cookie boards, Jack," said his mother, not missing a *beat*, *beat*, *beat* on the dough.

Jack unwrapped the carved wooden shapes— shepherd, star, camel, king, man and woman kneeling, baby, and cross. The last mold was an angel the size of his hand.

"It's so big!" Jack exclaimed. He could make a cookie like that last a whole week.

Jack's mother helped him roll the dough into a smooth oval. It was hard work.

"Why are we going to so much trouble to make Christmas cookies people are just going to eat anyway?" Jack asked.

His mom picked up the big angel mold and dusted it with flour. "Maybe it's time you heard why people first started making Christmas cookies."

Jack watched as his mother pressed the angel board into the dough. "The story goes back hundreds of years," she began, "back to the Middle Ages. In the Old Country—where your father's people lived—times were hard."

Jack rolled another batch of dough and wondered if times in the Middle Ages had been harder than they were right now, and if boys missed their fathers like he missed his.

The villagers couldn't afford school, so most couldn't read. As Christmas drew near, one family longed to help their neighbors discover the true meaning of Christmas.

"Let's carve figures to tell the story of Christ's birth!" the father, a woodcarver, suggested.

"But the villagers are hungry," his wife pointed out. "We should bake for them."

So the family worked together. The woodcarver whittled, scooping out wood until it formed the shape of an angel. He finished all the figures.

Then his wife mixed sweet dough to fill the molds.

When the cookies were done, the children decorated them with berries and colored sugar.

On Christmas Eve the woodcarver's family carried the cookies to the village. Soon a crowd gathered. As his daughter held up the angel cookie, the woodcarver began: "Long ago an angel like this one brought us the most wonderful news: 'Today in the town of David a Savior has been born to you; he is Christ the Lord.'"

They recounted the whole story of Jesus' life as they handed out cookies to the amazed listeners. Ever since that night, generations have passed down the art of making Christmas cookies and of telling the story of the true meaning of Christmas.

At the Christmas Eve service Jack thought of the woodcarver's family when the pastor read the same passage from Luke, the angel's announcement to the shepherds.

As Jack stood to sing "Hark! The Herald Angels Sing," his gaze fell on the stained-glass window. All of the figures were there—the star, the shepherd, Mary, Joseph, and baby Jesus. And above them was the angel. The window told the whole story, just like the Christmas cookies.

That night Jack dreamed
of giant Christmas cookies.
When he awoke, his
mother was waiting.
"Merry Christmas, Jack."
She handed him the big
angel cookie.

"For me?" Jack hugged
his mother. But before he
could take a bite, there was
a knock at the door.

Jack froze. His mother
raced past him to answer
the door. It would be just
like Dad to surprise them
and show up on Christmas
morning.

An old man stood in the doorway. "Could you spare a stranger a bite to eat?" he asked.

Disappointment choked off Jack's words and made his eyes water.

Jack could tell his mother was as let down as he was, but she invited the man to come in from the cold. "You're welcome to share our breakfast," she said.

The stranger ate fast without saying much. When he'd finished every last crumb, he thanked them and left.

Jack watched the man walk off toward the tracks. Jack hoped—prayed—that strangers had invited his dad to share their breakfast. Jack wished he'd taken the time to talk to the stranger, to wish him a Merry Christmas.

"Jack, don't forget your cookie," Mom said.

Jack ran his finger along the grooves of the angel's wings. He could almost hear the old woodcarver. "That's it!" he exclaimed.

Jack tore out of the house and ran to catch up with the stranger.

"What's this?" asked the stranger, taking the cookie Jack offered him.

"It's yours," Jack explained. "And there's a story that goes with it." Then right there, beside the railroad tracks, under a gray sky that promised snow, Jack began: "Long ago an angel like this one brought us the most wonderful news: 'Today in the town of David a Savior has been born to you; he is Christ the Lord.'"

# The Original Christmas Cookie

In the Schwaben region of Southern Germany, Austria, and Switzerland, cookie boards called springerle molds were carved by craftsmen into shapes. In the Middle Ages the shapes were mainly religious. These cookies are still made today either by pressing dough into a mold or by rolling out the dough and imprinting it with specially designed rolling pins.